D1247028

THE
ALLIGATOR
CASE

THE
ALLIGATOR
CASE

STORY AND PICTURES

BY

WILLIAM PÈNE DU BOIS

HARPER & ROW, PUBLISHERS · NEW YORK, EVANSTON, AND LONDON

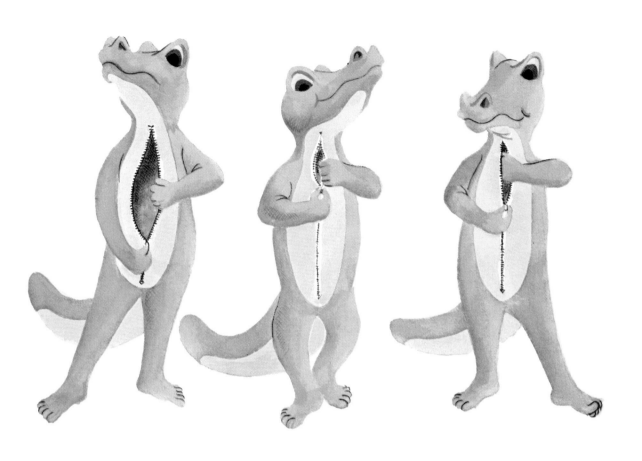

TO THE EXTRAORDINARY BALLANTINES, CIRCUS FAMILY—

BILL, ROBERTA, TOBY CIRCUS, TIM JOEY, TIA CLARA, BRIDGET MAMIE, AND LULU SUZANNE

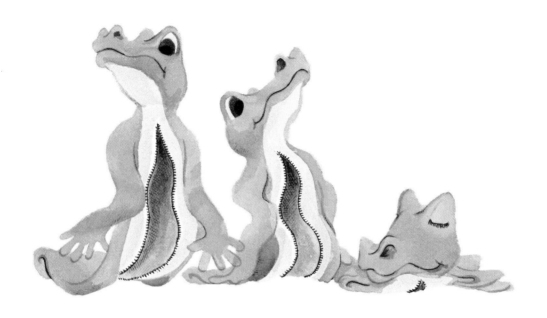

Contents

INTRODUCTION

I am a detective.

I may not be as old as I look.

It should be hard to tell how old I am, what I do, or even who I am, because I am a detective and should at all times pass undetected.

I must be shadowy and fade into the background.

I live in a small town with one hotel, one railroad station, one school, one athletic field, one gas station, and two stores—both general.

There is one policeman in the town. He is out of shape because there are no bad people to keep him moving. His name is Officer Dillingham.

I am a detective, and I often feel I live in the wrong place.

I look forward to weekends.

There is one train which visits my town.

It makes a stop Saturday morning coming from the East, and it makes another stop Sunday afternoon coming from the West.

It's the same train and it's my one hope for badmen.

I am a detective, and I must be alert and wide-awake on weekends.

One Friday a stranger roared into town bringing with him a great deal of noise and a cloud of dust. He was a big man in a small lemon-yellow sports car. He was wearing a derby hat with a tall crown, a black suit pinched at the waist, skinny tight trousers, and a lemon-yellow vest to match his car.

He stopped at Larkin's farm.

He exchanged a few words with Larkin, who is a man of few words, then placed a crisp green bill in Larkin's outstretched hand.

He took four poles with brass ends from the trunk of

his car. He screwed the poles together, making a long handle which in turn he screwed into a brush. He took a bucket of glue from the trunk and pasted five circus posters, one by one, on the street side of Larkin's barns.

He unscrewed and replaced his equipment, squeezed himself into the sports car, and roared away, taking with him his noise and dust cloud.

I didn't know it then, but these posters were to mark the unfolding of my first challenge.

I am a detective, and I refer to the singular events which were to follow as THE ALLIGATOR CASE.

THE
ALLIGATOR
CASE

MY TRAP-TRAP

I didn't know it then, but I had started working on The Alligator Case before the crimes were committed or the policeman was bitten in the line of duty.

The fresh five posters on Larkin's barns announced the performance at two P.M. Sunday of Leeds' Leading Circus. Its leading act featured a fierce alligator fired from a cannon into a tiny water tank. The alligator's name was ASTROGATOR.

I had no way of knowing if there were badmen in the circus, but ASTROGATOR looked terrible. He was wearing goggles, a crash helmet, and a grim grin. I decided at once that I must prepare a trap for him in case he should escape. I had no reason to believe he would escape, but I am a detective and had to suppose he might.

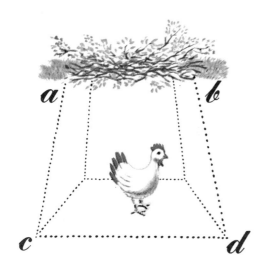

Dressed as a hunter, with shovel, pickax, and short ladder, I dug a hole for ASTROGATOR. I dug it near the river because I have reason to believe escaped alligators head for water. I dug a trap-trap because trap-traps are best. A trap-trap is a trap the cross section of which is trapezoidal, which means its base is parallel to its top but wider than its top. You cannot climb the walls of a trap-trap, because they lean toward you. I climbed out of my trap-trap with my short ladder and covered the hole with branches, twigs, and long grass. I left my short ladder in it, in case of accident before Sunday. Sunday morning I would put my chicken at the bottom of my trap-trap for bait and remove the short ladder. My chicken wouldn't like it, but I am a detective and must at times be severe.

At nine thirty-three P.M. on Friday, a little over five hours after the departure of the black and yellow stranger, I was already ready for ASTROGATOR.

16

BROMWELL, FISH, AND JOURNEY

Saturday morning, dressed as usual as a porter, I met the train.

The train always has three cars.

I know exactly where the middle car stops, and I stood at that point, eyes wide open, covering all doors. That Saturday there were three passengers, one from each car—two men and one lady.

The first man was carrying a strange case.

It was long and skinny.

At first glance I took it to be a case for fishing poles, but I am a detective and must not make easy guesses.

The case more likely was fitted out with poisoned spears, or a long snake stretched out straight. The other case he

carried looked standard enough but could have been filled with mice, guinea pigs, and other snake food.

The second man was tall and fat and was carrying what looked to be a bassoon case and a large suitcase. He was wearing a brown tweed jacket and red trousers with gold braid down the sides. He wore brown high shoes with thick soles. He could have been half-dressed as a bassoon-ist in a marching band—he seemed to want me to believe he was. I am a detective and must never be duped. A bazooka might find its way into a bassoon case.

The lady was carrying a light coat over her arm. This could have meant one of two things. She could have felt too warm to wear the coat, or have been hiding a daz-zling diamond bracelet because she had good reason to believe the other two passengers were crooks.

I was asked to carry the lady's suitcase, the large suit-case, and the bazooka case. The other man wished to carry his own snake and snake-food cases. I was asked to lead them to the hotel.

20

I stood near the desk long enough to hear their names and room numbers. Miss Journey was to take her enormous diamond bracelet to Room 2. Mr. Bromwell would share Room 3 with his snake and snake food, and Mr. Fish would march his army shoes, red trousers, and loaded bazooka and bazooka-rocket case into Room 1.

Miss Journey was to be sandwiched between badmen.

I would have liked to stay and keep a watchful eye on things in the hotel, but I am a detective, and the hotel manager says that detectives make his guests nervous.

I decided to change from my porter's suit to my old-man's suit and white beard and sit opposite the hotel and whittle the day away—unnoticed but noticing—whittling on a stick, like a hick.

The hotel served lunch at noon.

At twelve ten, walking old-man style, I hobbled stiffly across the street to peer in the dining-room window. Miss Journey, Mr. Bromwell, and Mr. Fish were seated in

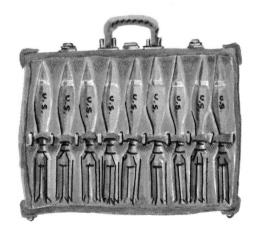

21

corners as far apart as possible. There was no talk between them, and each was busy with breaded veal cutlets, home fried potatoes, and creamed spinach. I returned to my bench and whittling.

Some time after lunch I heard lively bassoon music—jigs and sea chanties—coming from Mr. Fish's Room 1; then to my amazement I saw Miss Journey sitting in the window of the same Room 1, smiling and beating time by nodding her head.

Other than that nothing happened until two P.M.

At that time Mr. Bromwell appeared at the hotel entrance with the hotel manager. He had his snake case and was wearing hip boots. The hotel manager was pointing to the river. I presumed Mr. Bromwell was taking his snake for a swim and airing.

I decided I must follow him.

It was a difficult decision to make because it meant losing contact with Miss Journey, who was now clapping hands to Mr. Fish's bassoon. I had to follow Mr. Brom-well, though, because he might fall into ASTROGATOR's trap-trap.

I rather hoped he would.

This was wrong on my part because a man or a snake is innocent until proved guilty.

Mr. Bromwell opened his skinny case and took from it a fishing pole. He waded into the river in his hip boots, and in a short afternoon caught three trout. He then took a metal box from his skinny case, tied the box to the end of his fish line, and cast the box into the river, where it sank out of sight beneath a column of small rising bubbles. He next took his fishing pole and

hid it under a tree, marking a branch directly over it with a small red ribbon.

I had kept hidden from sight all afternoon, which was good. I remember thinking at the time that perhaps the silly fool thought this was a way to catch sardines.

He took his skinny case, three trout, and returned to the hotel.

I had lost contact with Miss Journey and Mr. Fish, which was stupid. I hurried back to my whittling bench.

At seven all three were in the dining room, though for this meal Miss Journey and Mr. Fish were seated together. The scene seemed serene, so I ran home for a quick supper of my own.

Nothing happened that night.

Summing up in bed, I concluded sadly that there was no snake after all. Along the same lines I reasoned that all my first guesses had been correct; Mr. Fish was really a bassoonist, and Miss Journey had felt too warm to wear her coat.

At one low point I was about to classify all three strangers as weekend visitors to my town, the bassoon-ist being a member of the Leeds' Leading Circus band who would rather travel by train than in a circus caravan.

Then I thought of the metal box on the end of Mr. Bromwell's fishing line.

Was he really that stupid a fisherman?

Did he really hope to catch sardines?

Of course not!

I had seen him catch three trout beautifully!

I shifted the great engines of my mind into high gear and re-examined my badmen.

It all became too clear.

Mr. Bromwell had already stolen Miss Journey's bracelet, and it was hidden in the metal box!

It would be picked up later, when the heat was off, after the policeman had failed to find either the bracelet or its robber.

As for Mr. Fish, he was a fat musical decoy, distracting poor Miss Journey with happy tunes while his partner robbed her room.

How stupid I had been not to have seen through them sooner!

I decided to do something about them at once!

Unfortunately, I fell asleep.

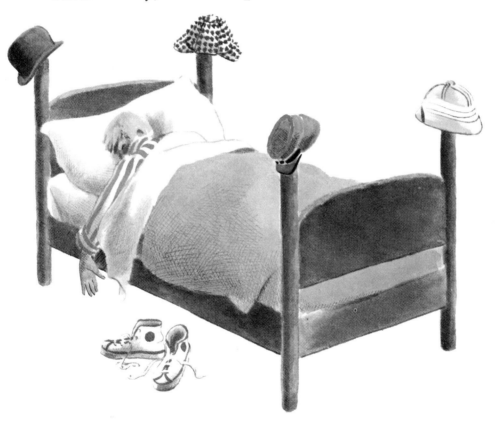

PORK CHOPS AND PEAS

Sunday morning I was up at dawn.

Cleverly dressed as a barefoot boy with cheeks of tan, I carelessly chewed on a piece of grass while humming "Turkey in the Straw."

With my straw hat balanced on my tousled hair, my patched dungarees half-suspended by half a suspender, my tree-branch fishing pole with laundry string and bent pin, I headed for the river.

A bowser-hound named Rover completed my bumpkin disguise. Also a fine actor, he was wagging his shaggy tail as though life were an endless procession of bones and possum hunts.

I was off to wrap up a robbery case.

That evening I would be a hero.

One sour note shattered my carefree elation. It was Mother reminding me that it was Sunday, that I had my usual chores, and to please stop my incessant day-dreaming.

"Incessant daydreaming" indeed! Behind every great man, as the saying goes, there's a woman telling him he's a nut-errant with his head in orbit.

Well, I'd show her!

Arriving at the river's edge, I quickly found the little red ribbon marking Mr. Bromwell's well-hidden fishing pole. Making certain I had been neither followed nor observed, I reeled in the metal box, confident I'd find Miss Journey's bracelet inside, the sparkling goods needed to clamp Bromwell and Fish in the clink.

It wasn't even locked.

My fingers shook and my heart pounded!

I was shocked to find that I wasn't cooler face to face with my moment of truth.

I was shocked even more when I opened the box and found it empty.

My great case collapsed before my popping eyes.

I lowered the empty metal box back down its column of rising bubbles and sadly returned home. I changed into my Sunday suit and headed for the athletic field to watch the circus tent go up.

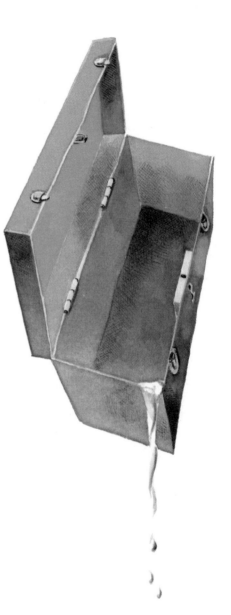

The raising of a circus tent is a fine sight to behold, and though I may seem worldly, it gets me every time. Elephants, each with a long rope tied to its collar, walk away from the center pole, pulling their ropes straight out like rays from the sun or the spokes of a wire wheel. The ponderous canvas mass goes straight up, *whoosh*, with a great sucking of air. And there—where there was nothing—is a big fat tent.

I am a detective, and I applied for a job with the circus so that I could keep an eye out for badmen.

You may wonder how a detective can keep his interest in his work so razor sharp.

It isn't easy.

After my great disappointment you might expect an easing of interest. Not for a moment! I am a detective and as relentless as a bird of prey.

On with the hunt!

I was offered one of two jobs—selling cotton candy or popcorn. Both jobs were good because they would allow me to circulate freely in and out of the tent and observe everything. I chose popcorn because it is less showy than cotton candy. I am a detective, and I work better when I do not attract attention. I also asked for and received an unpopped handful of popcorn for my chicken, who would soon be feeling in the dumps deep in my alligator trap-trap.

I baited my trap-trap with my chicken, covered it over, and hid the short ladder up a tree. I returned to town and went to church, where I pass the plate.

Lunch at the hotel after church is the big Sunday event in my town.

There are so many guests, there are two services—the first at twelve and the second at one.

Dressed as a busboy, I work both services and miss nothing. I could be dressed as a waiter, but again everybody in a restaurant looks at waiters and tries to catch their eyes. Nobody looks at busboys. As a busboy I can look at everybody and not be looked at in return.

I was surprised, at the second service, to see Miss Journey seated with Mr. Bromwell, a new combination. They were at a table near the cash register and the door into the hall.

Then Mr. Fish made his entrance.

He had reserved a table in the center of the dining room.

For the first time since arriving, he was completely dressed in red and gold, with frogs and epaulets. At previous meals he had been quiet and discreet. That Sunday he was loud and vulgar. He made rude noises and spoke only in commands.

I kept a careful watch on him.

Sunday lunch is always the same at the hotel. There is a choice of shrimp cocktail or fruit cup, of roast beef or roast turkey. There is a choice of baked or mashed potatoes, peas and carrots or string beans. There is a choice of apple or blueberry pie. I list this dreary information only in view of what happened that Sunday.

I was duped, fooled, stupidly taken in.

30

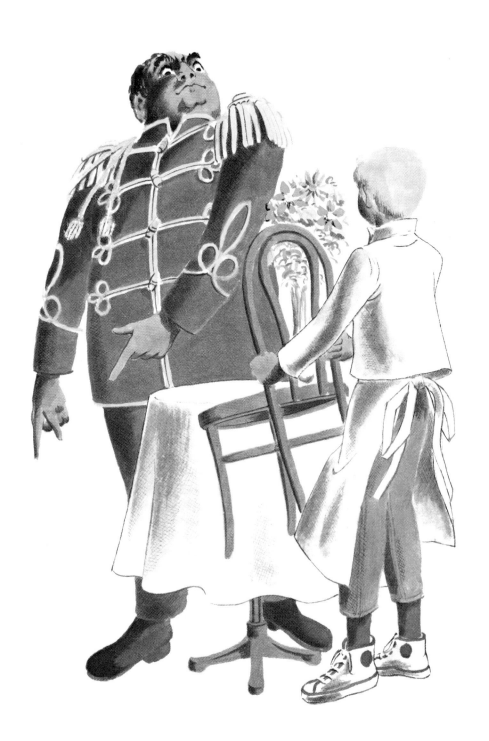

I am a detective, and I cannot forgive myself.

Mr. Fish first ordered me to remove all knives and forks and glassware, and to leave only two teaspoons on his table. He thus at the start captured my attention.

I blush at the memory of it all.

He next shouted "WAITER!" so loudly all conversation ceased.

A waiter rushed to his table.

"Yes, sir, would you prefer the shrimp cocktail or the fresh fruit cup?"

"Skip it!" bellowed Mr. Fish.

"Yes, sir. Now then, the roast beef is blood rare, or do you wish the turkey?"

"I want pork chops well-done, and bullet peas!"

"Sorry, sir..."

"And paper panties on the pork chops!"

"Sorry, sir..."

"By bullet peas, I mean green peas hard and firm that bounce!"

"Sorry, sir, but on Sundays..."

"Stop being sorry and bring me my order!"

"It will take time, it will have to be cooked to ord—"

"Get out of here!"

"Yes, sir."

Needless to say, there was nervous tension in the dining room and stunned silence broken only by the clitter-clatter of silverware and china. The uneasiness resulted in rapid eating. The Sunday feast turned into a joyless race. Most guests had finished their meals and paid their checks before Mr. Fish was served; but they sat transfixed, rather afraid to stay but too afraid to leave and miss something horrible.

In came the overdone pork chops with paper panties, and the bullet peas. The waiter, shaking noticeably, placed them in front of the fat red-and-gold bassoonist.

Mr. Fish studied his plate.

He picked up a pea and rolled it between thumb and forefinger.

He smiled. "Good, good. Not bad at all."

His change of mood relaxed the charged atmosphere of the room.

Guests who had been sitting stiffly in a conscious effort to mind their own business unbent a bit and risked a peek at Mr. Fish.

Mr. Fish placed a teaspoon on each side of his plate, with its handle pointed forward. He placed a pea on the handle of the spoon near his left hand and picked up a pork chop with his right by its paper panty.

He thumped down with his left fist on the bowl of the spoon, catapulting the bullet pea high in the air.

As the pea passed his enormous open mouth he batted it in with his overdone pork chop.

A small boy in the room, overwhelmed with boorish joy at this terrible display of table manners, stood up and let escape a piercing "HOORAY!" He received a stinging slap from his mother for his efforts.

Seemingly unaware of more and more eyes staring bluntly at him, Mr. Fish repeated the feat, then did it again, and again, and again.

He never missed.

Placing a pea on the handle of each teaspoon, thumping the peas up close to the ceiling, quickly picking up a pork chop in each hand, he batted two peas into his mouth!

He smiled to himself at the success of the double action, smacked his lips, then followed up with an encore.

Guests and waiters, at first cowed and apart, slowly grouped around his table, mouths open in utter disbelief,

and looking oddly as though they too hoped to catch a
batted bullet pea—a foul ball off the pork-chop handle.

But he never missed.

As the peas vanished two by two he made the trick
still harder by taking a bite of pork chop between hits,
shrinking his bats.

And he never missed.

"Why?" I asked myself. "Why all this?"

A cold shudder ran down my spine.

Who was watching the cash register?

Not the cashier—she was standing next to me.

I pushed my way through the guests and waiters now crowding Mr. Fish's table.

I leapt over the cashier's desk.

The register's drawer was out like a Ubangi's lower lip, gaping empty, bare as a bone!

THE BIG BITE

Early this morning I thought I had solved the case of the stolen diamond bracelet.

Then I found I had no case at all.

Right after lunch I had a big hotel robbery case, and when I should have been in hot pursuit of suspects, what was I doing?

Washing dishes.

Oh, the shame of it all!

I am a detective, and when I pretend to be a busboy, I'm a busboy all the way. I cannot afford to lose an important observation post for future cases.

After I discovered the theft, there was wild excitement.

The cashier burst into tears, then fainted dead away. She was revived with smelling salts and carried to her room so that she might cry some more in private.

The policeman, at the time of the crime, was already in his front-row-center seat at the circus, waiting to be entertained. He refused to believe there had been a robbery.

It was unfortunate but true that every year the policeman and the hotel manager fought over sitting in the front-row-center seat. The childishness of such behavior was now only too apparent. The policeman usually got there first, being less busy than the hotel manager, and then the hotel manager tried to trick him out of it with false alarms.

"I'll look into it right after the circus," the policeman said, laughing. "Ha, ha, yes. *After* the circus, come and see me about your robbery." He clamped a tight grip on each chair handle and wedged his round body firmly into a position of dead weight. "Bring on the clowns!" he shouted. "First things first!"

"But I'm telling the truth this time! I've been robbed! Ask anyone!"

"Sure you have," the policeman said smugly.

When in a fit of desperation the hotel manager tried to hoist the policeman out of his seat, he laughed louder. "Tickling will get you nowhere," he snorted. "This is my seat! The early bird catches the worm! Elephants won't budge me!"

"You're an elephant yourself, you fat pig!"

"Ha, ha!" The policeman pointed upward and backward with his thumbs. "Go sit in the peanut gallery where *you* belong!"

Meanwhile, sweat pouring from my brow, up to my elbows in suds, I reviewed the crime and planned my attack. I was dealing with a smoothly trained trio. Mr. Fish had put on a show while Mr. Bromwell and Miss Journey calmly emptied the cash register and walked away, pockets bulging. Neither Mr. Bromwell nor Miss

Journey were in the dining room at the time the robbery was discovered.

But I was just guessing this to be true.

Having been fooled with the others, I had no evidence.

Right after shouting, "WE'VE BEEN ROBBED!" I was about to arrest Mr. Fish for making a distraction to cover a theft. But he made it impossible with a clever speech. Batting his last two bullet peas into his mouth with two skinny pork-chop bones in paper panties, he announced: "Ladies and Gentlemen, I hope you will accept kindly this tiny sample of the sort of varied and extraordinary entertainment you may expect this afternoon at Leeds' Leading Circus. I thank you."

Such an eloquent alibi was hard to challenge.

To make things worse, a burst of applause was awarded the bad-mannered crook!

He cleared a path through his admirers and marched grandly out of the dining room, heading upstairs.

Happy to see the last of the dishes out of the drier and back on their shelves, I patted my red hands dry and headed for the circus.

Not knowing the policeman was pinned to his seat by his own stubbornness, I pictured him as being in the process of arresting Mr. Bromwell and Miss Journey.

The hotel seemed deserted. Most everyone had left for the circus. I was racing in that direction when I heard a strange thrashing sound coming from upstairs, along with rhythmic grunts and groans. There followed the sound of furniture being knocked about the room. I stopped in my tracks and ran up the back stairs and out on the balcony. I crawled to the window of Room 1, where the noise seemed loudest.

I peeked inside.

I saw a fat alligator dancing the twist in front of a full-length mirror.

Rubbing my eyes and looking again, the alligator proved to be someone in an alligator suit, and by the size of the person, Mr. Fish.

There was a black thread attached from his left fore-paw to his lower jaw, and another black thread attached from his right forepaw to his great tail, so that when he twisted, his mouth snapped open and shut and his tail lashed to and fro, knocking over chairs, table, and hat rack.

It was a delightful sight.

I was staring at him when he suddenly turned and looked directly at me.

There is nothing quite as embarrassing as being caught in such a situation, and I felt my face flush red and my ears burn bright.

The alligator merely bowed, and I crawled away in shame.

It is at times unfortunate that one cannot arrest rob-bers unless one either catches them in the act or with the stolen goods on them. Due to stupidity I had not seen them commit the crime and had to catch them with the goods. It would not be easy. I am a detective, and I must stay calm, be precise, and THINK!

I assumed Mr. Fish would be going to the circus in an alligator suit, so I ran ahead to jump into my popcorn hat and observe. It was high time to show my stuff and become a hero.

The circus program opened with a spectacle, or as circus people pronounce it, "speck-tackle" with the *tackle* pronounced like a football lineman, or with a hat on the â.

This sort of silly information rattles around in the brains of detectives.

I am a detective and might someday be looking for a circus clown badman. If I thought I saw my suspect but was not certain it was he without his wig, red nose, and baggy pants, I might ask him if he'd ever seen an Army--Navy football game, a Tournament of Roses, or some such pageant. If he answered, "Yes. What a speck-tâckle!" I'd slap on the cuffs and lock him up.

The opening speck-tâckle was in honor of Leeds' Leading Circus' star performer, ASTROGATOR: "Egypt's Prehistoric Entry into the Space Race."

It was a grand opening!

The entire human cast of the company, including the band, entered in alligator suits and performed such fine dances as the Chomp, the Green Bottom, the Slither, the Crocodero, and the Big Mouth. The enormous arena, big enough for three rings, was filled with romping alligators. The lashing of their tails fanned the summer air with breezes. The clouds of sawdust which enveloped them made an effect of a desert storm along the banks of the Nile.

44

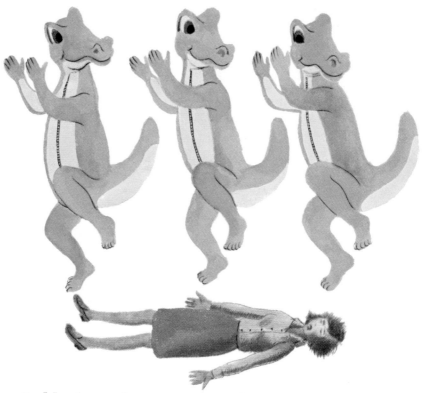

Suddenly, in the center ring, there appeared a screaming woman with such a terrible look on her face that she brought silence to what had been a riotous scene. In a voice which filled the tent, she bellowed: "I'VE BEEN ROBBED. ALL MY RECEIPTS ARE GONE!"

She then fainted.

It was a big day for fainting cashiers.

The policeman, at long last roused to some sense of emergency, pried himself loose from his front-row-center seat. He plowed a path to the cashier's booth, and holding back the curious, flung open the door. An alligator was seated at the window. Grabbing his handcuffs with one hand, and the alligator's paw with the other, he announced in majestic tones, "I PLACE YOU UNDER ARREST!" Unfortunately, and odd as it may seem, the alligator at the cashier's window was a real animal, none other than ASTROGATOR himself, the circus' shooting star.

In better training and faster on the draw, ASTRO-GATOR promptly gave the policeman a severe bite on the arm.

Seeing blood, his own blood, the policeman too fainted dead away.

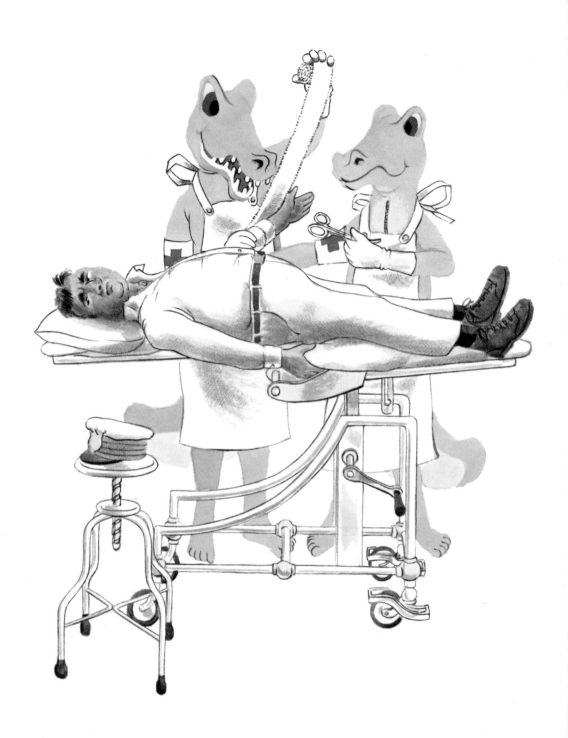

HAYSEED IN ACTION

ASTROGATOR's two trainers, both in alligator suits for the speck-tâckle, subdued their star attraction and flipped him into a cage on wheels, parked near the cashier's booth. They next carried the policeman to the circus' hospital trailer.

There too the doctor and nurse were found to be in alligator suits.

Bandaged, revived, and boiling angry, the policeman revealed the brilliance promised thirty-seven years earlier when he received his first badge and whistle at Police Officers' Training School: "Bring me the cashier!"

"Yes, sir."

"Cashier, did you see the robber?"

"Yes, there were three of them."

"Armed?"

"One gun."

"Did you recognize any or all of them?"

"They were in alligator suits."

"Did you recognize their voices?"

"No, sir. They were speaking in falsetto voices."

"Male falsetto or female falsetto?"

"Both."

"What did they do with the money?"

"Split it. They made three big piles. They had trouble with their paws."

"What did they do then?"

"One of them said, 'Stash it in your tails, and back to the big tent!'"

"AHA! Thank you."

"May I go?"

"Yes, but don't leave the area."

The policeman took his circus program from his hip pocket. "Now then," he shouted, "it says here there are '90 Alligators 90 in a Sentimental Tribute to the Twist.' I want all 90 Alligators 90 to line up in six rows of fifteen alligators each. I want all alligators in formation like soldiers, ON THE DOUBLE!" He clapped his hands, blew his whistle, took his service revolver from its holster, and spun its chamber. "One false move and POW! ON THE DOUBLE! SQUARE OFF, YOU ALLIGATORS!"

They were soon in fairly tight formation, six rows of fifteen, all ninety present and accounted for.

"Now then," the policeman resumed, "you are going to strip off your alligator suits one at a time, at my command, and you are going to take those alligator suits and turn them inside out, right down to the tips of their tails, and shake them out, do you understand?"

There was a chorus of affirmative grunts.

The search started.

Each circus performer was in full costume under his alligator suit.

It was a great sight, like unwrapping green Christmas packages. An alligator would unzip from throat to navel and out would pop a clown, a trapeze artist, an equestrian, or a ringmaster.

50

The audience was in a nervous, munching mood, and I soon sold six trays of popcorn.

I am a detective, and as I stood there watching in my popcorn hat I was about to solve The Alligator Case.

I wanted to see just one member of the band, one circus musician.

I think the first one to be unwrapped was alligator Number 26. He was dressed in a sky-blue uniform with white frogs and braid.

I dashed down to the arena and up to the policeman.

"Excuse me, sir."

"Get lost, young fella!"

"If your search fails, I think I can promise you the three robbers, the hotel money, and the circus money delivered to you under the big tree by the river."

The policeman seemed ready to explode with fury. I did not care. I just wanted him to hear my message.

"GET LOST!"

"Yes, sir. Under the BIG TREE. By the RIVER! Four thirty P.M.!"

"OUT! OUT! GET OUT!"

I returned my popcorn hat and empty tray and ran home. I put on my porter's suit and ran to the hotel. The Sunday train leaves my town at four twenty-five. If my thinking had been correct, I'd find Mr. Bromwell, Miss Journey, and Mr. Fish in the hotel bar, laughing and chatting.

I entered the hotel.

Mr. Bromwell, Miss Journey, and Mr. Fish were in the hotel bar, laughing and chatting.

I am a detective, and I was about to play my big scene.

I took a deep breath and collected myself.

Standing in the barroom doorway, I spoke to Mr. Bromwell, Miss Journey, and Mr. Fish. "The Sunday train leaves at four twenty-five. I hope you had a profitable visit."

"Very profitable, young man," said Miss Journey.

Mr. Fish chuckled.

"Why did he use that word?" muttered Mr. Bromwell.

"What word?"

"Profitable."

"It's just hick talk," said Miss Journey, smiling at me.

"I think he knows something!"

"No hick knows anything," said Miss Journey, still smiling at me.

"I've come for your luggage."

"It's in the lobby. We're all paid up and ready to go."

I looked at my watch. "I think we should start for the station now."

"But of course! We're off, young man, we're off!"

I was allowed to carry all of the luggage on the trip back to the station, so I wheeled it in the hotel's luggage cart. It was a two-minute walk to the station, and the train was due in five minutes.

"I hope you enjoyed your trout," I offered.

Mr. Bromwell nearly screamed. "What trout? Who said anything about trout?"

I am a detective and was now in high gear. "Oh, sir, I'm a busboy on Sundays, and the cook at the hotel told me he cooked each of you a trout for breakfast."

"Oh."

"He said you caught them yourself. Could you please tell me the bend of the river where you fished? I fish too, sometimes. I would like to know the *exact* spot; it makes a difference, I'm told."

Mr. Bromwell's mouth fell open.

I could hear the train approaching. As the smoke from the locomotive rose on the horizon it seemed to me a red flush rose up Mr. Bromwell's neck.

He turned again to Miss Journey. "I tell you this hayseed knows something!"

The train clanged into the station and came to a steamy stop.

"Well, I hope to see you all again soon," I said. I stood on one side of the luggage cart, separating myself from Mr. Bromwell, Miss Journey, and Mr. Fish. "And from time to time, I'll check that metal box in the river for you, to see if you've caught anything else."

"GRAB HIM!" Bromwell bellowed.

I am a detective, and I can outrun crooks any day. I sprinted for the river with the robbers panting at my heels. I needed space between us, so I put on a burst of reserve speed. Arriving at the river, I was overwhelmed with joy to see the policeman seated under the big tree, his jacket off and shirt sleeve rolled up, checking his alligator bite. He looked discouraged.

"HERE THEY COME!" I shouted to him.

The policeman jumped to his feet.

I ran to the little red ribbon, dove for the hidden fishing pole, reeled in the metal box, and dragged it at the end of the pole over the river bank. The three robbers had caught up and were hot on my heels.

I am a detective, and I nimbly jumped over my trap-trap, purposely dropping the fishing pole.

Mr. Bromwell, Miss Journey and Mr. Fish dove for the metal box like football players after a fumble.

CAUTION
COKE PIT

All three belly flopped into my trap-trap.
Out popped my chicken.
I caught her in my hands. She lost a few feathers.
The robbers in my trap-trap, caught with the goods

58

on them, were snarling at each other like animals.

I introduced them to the policeman.

He made his arrest.

I am a detective, and The Alligator Case was solved.

WRAP-UP

Dressed as a schoolboy, I returned to school Monday morning for another dreary week.

I am a detective, and I look forward to weekends.

Sunday evening I received a one hundred dollar reward from the hotel, a two hundred dollar reward from the circus, and a two hundred dollar reward from the mayor of my town. All of this money was presented to me at a dinner in my honor at the hotel.

I even made a ridiculous speech, documented with photographs, after which there were many questions about the case.

Most people seemed to think Mr. Bromwell, Miss Journey, and Mr. Fish were with the circus. They were not. They had planned the robbery carefully and brought their own alligator suits. I too thought they might be with the circus until I saw the blue musician uniform under the alligator suit. Mr. Fish wore a red uniform.

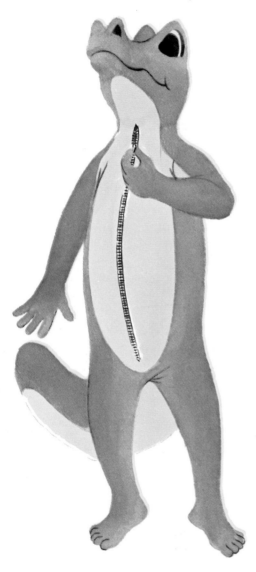

Making people think they were three of the 90 Alligators 90 gave them time to hide the money in the river while the real 90 Alligators 90 were being searched under the watchful eyes of everybody in town. They hid the money in the river because they were afraid they might be searched too. The money was to be picked up much later, when the robbery would be more or less forgotten. The money was carefully sealed in rubber tobacco pouches.

If I had felt they were leaving town with the money, I would have had them searched at the next station by having our station-master send a wire; but when Mr. Bromwell became so excited about the trout, I knew the metal box was the hiding place.

I do not know how ASTRO-GATOR found himself in the cashier's booth.

I suppose he was waiting outside the big tent in his cage on wheels, listening for his cue.

Seeing him there after their rob-

bery, when the cashier ran screaming into the big tent, Mr. Bromwell,
Miss Journey, and Mr. Fish prob-
ably thought it a finishing touch
to a slick crime to wheel ASTRO-
GATOR to the booth and make
him the suspect.

Mr. Bromwell, Miss Journey,
and Mr. Fish are now caged them-
selves.

The mayor spoke at my dinner.
He seemed to know me only for
the kind of job I do mowing his
lawn.

My schoolteacher spoke at my
dinner too. She said I had great
potential but was an incessant day-
dreamer (those words again). She
said, "He's the classic example of
an absentminded student." I
found the remark amusing.

A long and somewhat silly news-
paper article Monday morning
pictured me as a model boy known
to everyone in my town for "the
unbelievable number of jobs he
undertakes in order to support his
mother, a widow."

One more thing.

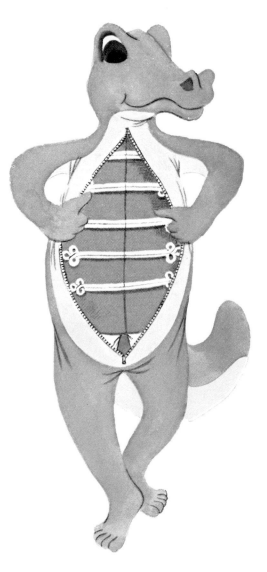

. . . . . A SKY BLUE MUSICIAN

63

I was asked what I would like to eat at a dinner in my honor. To my own stupefaction I heard myself answer, "Overdone pork chops with paper panties, and bullet peas."

I am happy to report I wasn't busboy for that party. The dining room was a MESS!